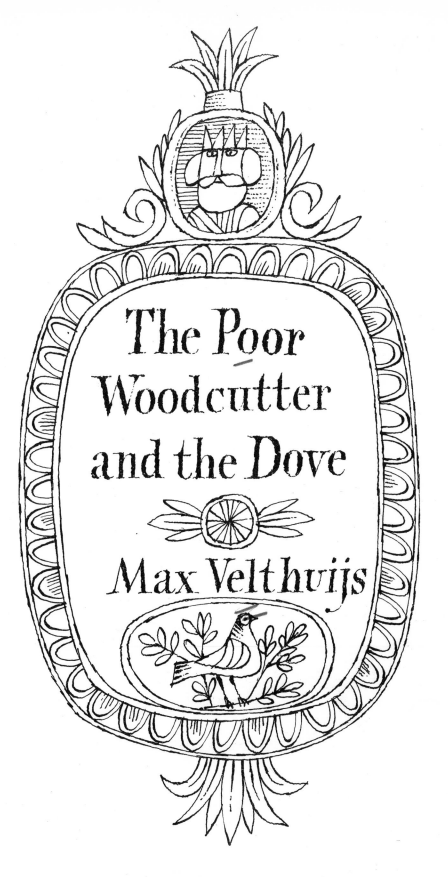

The Poor Woodcutter and the Dove

Max Velthuijs

A Seymour Lawrence Book
Delacorte Press / New York

The Poor Woodcutter and the Dove was adapted by
Max Velthuijs from a story by the Brothers Grimm.

Copyright © Nord-Sud Verlag, Switzerland
First published in English in Great Britain
by Abelard-Schuman Ltd, 8 King Street, London WC.2
English translation Copyright© 1970 by Abelard-Schuman Ltd.
All rights reserved. No part of this book may be
reproduced in any form or by any means without the prior
written permission of the Publisher, excepting brief
quotes used in connection with reviews written specifically
for inclusion in a magazine or newspaper.
Library of Congress Catalog Card Number: 79-125037
Color separation by Photolitho AG, Switzerland
Printed in Holland by Meijer Wormerveer n.v.
First American Edition

To all children who would like to be king.

Once upon a time there was a poor woodcutter. He lived with his wife in a little hut.

One day he went to the forest with
his axe to look for a big tree to cut down.

After he had worked for a while, he became tired and hungry. He sat down to rest, and looking up at the trees, he saw some beautiful doves.

The woodcutter was hungry and ran home to get a gun, so that he could shoot a dove for the cooking pot.

But he did not hit a single bird. They all flew away. Only one came back, glided down to the woodcutter and sat on his gun, saying: "If you promise never to shoot at doves again, you may wish for anything that will bring you peace and happiness." The poor woodcutter was very surprised but he gave his promise. He wished for a better house and more money.

When he returned to the place where his little hut had been, he saw a beautiful house. His wife was standing at the door with a smile on her face.

They lived happily and had nothing to worry about but, after a while, the woodcutter became dissatisfied. He wanted a big castle, beautiful clothes and horses. He ran into the wood, called the dove and told her his wishes.

When he returned home, he saw a wonderful castle where the house had been. His wife, dressed in beautiful clothes, came to a window to welcome him.

For some time he was a happy man. He was rich and power-ful, and the peasants in the neighbourhood treated him with respect. But once again he grew dissatisfied, and went into the wood, called the dove and asked her to make him a king.

Once he was king, he felt even more powerful. He forced the peasants to pay heavy taxes on their land and they paid, because they were afraid of him. Thus he became very, very rich, but still he was not satisfied. He was a king, but there were other rulers besides him, and he wanted to become king of all kings.

He chose the strongest men
from among his peasants and formed
an army.

With this army he surrounded the castle of a neighbouring king whom he was determined to conquer. But he was received with a hail of bullets and arrows. His soldiers, who had never been asked to fight before, threw down their weapons and ran back to their farms.

The king was very angry. He climbed the tower of his castle, called the dove, and said: "Give me a great army with well-armed men so that I shall have power over everyone. Only then will I be satisfied."

"No," said the dove. "I have given you everything you needed to live in peace and happiness. Now you are asking for something that will bring you neither." She flew upward, and settled on the roof of the castle.

The king was mad with rage. He ordered his men to shoot a cannon at the dove. The cannon balls struck the castle again and again but always missed the dove. Finally, the whole castle burned to the ground and the woodcutter's riches were destroyed with it.

He became a poor woodcutter again. Where the castle once stood, there was only a little hut. Every day he went to the wood where the dove lived. He cut down trees so that he could earn enough money to buy food for himself and his wife. With that he had to be satisfied.